# TOUGH TRUCKS
## The Bulldozer

By Nancy Parent
Illustrated by David Desforges and Bill Alger

SCH... ...lic Library
New York  Toronto ...y
Mexico City  New ... ...048

ISBN 0-439-36638-0

10 9 8 7 6 5                    04 05 06

Cover design by Maria Stasavage
Interior design by Bethany Dixon

Printed in the U.S.A.
First printing, March 2003

# Dear Family Members:

Welcome to the Tonka Tough Trucks series! Your child will have the opportunity to learn more about how things work while improving reading skills. I know that kids like trucks because they are big and interesting. They also enjoy big and interesting words like the ones in this book. Tonka truck books provide an introduction to nonfiction text—the kind of writing your child will meet in textbooks and even on the Internet. Here are suggestions for helping your child *before*, *during*, and *after* reading.

## Before

- Look at the cover and pictures and have your child predict what the story is about.
- Be word watchers. Look for new and challenging vocabulary and talk about what the words mean.

## During

- Encourage your child to use phonics skills to sound out new words.
- Provide the word for your child, especially when it is a technical one, when more assistance is needed so that he or she does not struggle and the experience of reading with you is a positive one.

## After

- Have your child keep lists of interesting and favorite words—there are so many choices in this book.
- Encourage your child to read the book over and over again. Brothers, sisters, grandparents, and even teddy bears make a great audience. Repeated readings develop confidence in young readers.
- Talk about the stories. Ask and answer questions.
- Visit a construction site and practice using new vocabulary words.

I do hope that you and your child enjoy the big trucks, big words, and big ideas in this book!

—Francie Alexander
Chief Academic Officer
Scholastic Education

They push everything out of the way. *Watch out!*

Dozers are the superheroes
of construction vehicles.

This scoops up dirt and rocks and flattens the ground like a pancake.

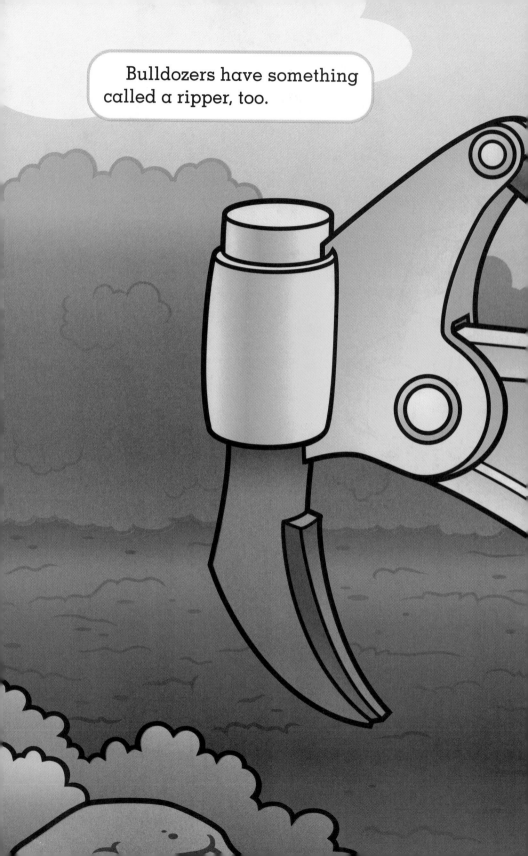

A bulldozer has two belt-shaped crawlers instead of tires.

An army tank has crawlers, too!

These are called spurs. They help break up really hard surfaces.

These are called dozer shovels.

The dozer shovel loads
soil onto a truck.

Watch that bucket dozer dump the dirt!

Bulldozers can roll across rough, tough surfaces.

To work the crawlers, you use hand levers or foot pedals.

. . . one crawler moves forward
while the other moves backward.

There are different kinds of dozers, too! Watch a swamp bulldozer at work.

This dozer's crawlers are really wide and long.

BAY 1    BAY 2

A trimming dozer works inside
containers on freighter ships.

Its blade scoops up steel, coal, sugar, or flour.

So get out of the way when you see
a bulldozer coming . . .
. . . unless you're in the driver's seat!